PLAY RHYMES

collected and illustrated by

MARC BROWN

E. P. DUTTON · NEW YORK

Permission to reprint the music for the following play rhymes, on pages 30–32, is gratefully acknowledged:

"The Crocodile" From *Ring Around the Moon* by Edith Fowke, © 1977. Reprinted by permission of the publisher Prentice-Hall, Inc., Englewood Cliffs, N.J. And used by permission of The Canadian Publishers, McClelland and Stewart, Toronto.

"Do Your Ears Hang Low?" From *Sally Go Round the Sun* by Edith Fowke. Used by permission of The Canadian Publishers, McClelland and Stewart, Toronto.

"I'm a Little Teapot" Copyright © 1974 by Oak Publications, A Div. of Music Sales Corp. International Copyright Secured. All Rights Reserved. Used by permission.

"John Brown's Baby" Reprinted by permission of Sterling Publishing Co., Inc., Two Park Avenue, New York, N.Y. 10016 from *The Best Singing Games for Children of All Ages* by Edgar S. Bley, © 1957 by Sterling Publishing Co., Inc.

"The Noble Duke of York" From *Sally Go Round the Moon, and Other Revels Songs and Singing Games for Young Children,* compiled by Nancy and John Langstaff.

"Wheels on the Bus" Copyright © 1974 by Oak Publications, A Div. of Music Sales Corp. International Copyright Secured. All Rights Reserved. Used by permission.

Library of Congress Cataloging-in-Publication Data
Brown, Marc Tolon. Play rhymes.
A collection of twelve play rhymes with illustrations
to demonstrate the accompanying finger plays or physical
activities. Includes music for the six rhymes
which are also songs.
1. Finger play—Juvenile literature.   2. Nursery
rhymes—Juvenile literature.   3. Songs—Juvenile literature.
[1. Finger play.   2. Nursery rhymes.   3. Songs.]
I. Title.
GV1218.F5B77   1987   793.4   87-13537
ISBN 0-525-44336-3

Published in the United States by E. P. Dutton,
2 Park Avenue, New York, N.Y. 10016,
a division of NAL Penguin Inc.
Published simultaneously in Canada by
Fitzhenry & Whiteside Limited, Toronto
Editor: Ann Durell   Designer: Riki Levinson
Printed in Hong Kong by South China Printing Co.
First Edition   COBE   10 9 8 7 6 5 4 3 2

for our newest playmate,
ELIZA MORGAN BROWN

Contents

John Brown's Baby

 John Brown's baby had a cold upon its chest,

 John Brown's baby had a cold upon its chest,

 John Brown's baby had a cold upon its chest,

And they rubbed it with camphorated oil.

The Counting Game

 One, two, buckle my shoe;

 Three, four, knock at the door;

 Five, six, pick up sticks;

 Seven, eight, stand up straight;

 Nine, ten, ring Big Ben;

 Eleven, twelve, dig and delve.

Do Your Ears Hang Low?

Do your ears hang low?

Do they wobble to and fro?

Can you tie them in a knot?

Can you tie them in a bow?

Can you throw them over your shoulder

Like a continental soldier?

Do your ears hang low?

The Noble Duke of York

 Oh, the noble Duke of York,

He had ten thousand men;

He marched them up to the top of the hill,

And he marched them down again.

Now when they were up, they were up;

And when they were down, they were down;

 But when they were only halfway up,

They were neither up nor down.

The Crocodile

 She sailed away on a happy summer day,

 On the back of a crocodile.

 "You'll see," said she,

 "he's as tame as tame can be;

 I'll ride him down the Nile."

 The croc winked his eye

 as she bade them all good-bye,

 Wearing a happy smile.

At the end of the ride,

the lady was inside,

And the smile on the crocodile.

Teddy Bear

 Teddy Bear, Teddy Bear, turn around.

 Teddy Bear, Teddy Bear, touch the ground.

 Teddy Bear, Teddy Bear, show your shoe.

 Teddy Bear, Teddy Bear, that will do!

 Teddy Bear, Teddy Bear, go upstairs.

 Teddy Bear, Teddy Bear, say your prayers.

 Teddy Bear, Teddy Bear, turn off the light.

 Teddy Bear, Teddy Bear, say good-night.

My Bicycle

One wheel, two wheels, on the ground,

My feet make the pedals go round and round.

Handlebars help me steer so straight,

Down the sidewalk, through the gate.

Elephant

Right foot, left foot, see me go.

I am gray and big and slow.

I come walking down the street

With my trunk and four big feet.

Bears, Bears, Everywhere

 Bears, bears, everywhere!

Climbing stairs

Sitting on chairs

Collecting fares

Painting squares

Bears, bears, everywhere!

Animals

 Can you hop like a rabbit?

 Can you jump like a frog?

 Can you walk like a duck?

 Can you run like a dog?

 Can you fly like a bird?

 Can you swim like a fish?

And be still like a good child—

As still as this?

Wheels on the Bus

 The wheels on the bus go round and round,

Round and round, round and round.

The wheels on the bus go round and round,

All through the town.

 The driver on the bus says, "Move on back,

Move on back, move on back."

The driver on the bus says, "Move on back,"

All through the town.

 The children on the bus say, "Yak yak yak,

Yak yak yak, yak yak yak."

The children on the bus say, "Yak yak yak,"

All through the town.

The mommies on the bus say, "Shh shh shh,

Shh shh shh, shh shh shh."

The mommies on the bus say, "Shh shh shh,"

All through the town.

I'm a Little Teapot

I'm a little teapot, short and stout.

Here is my handle, here is my spout.

When I start to steam up, then I shout,

Tip me over and pour me out.

John Brown's Baby

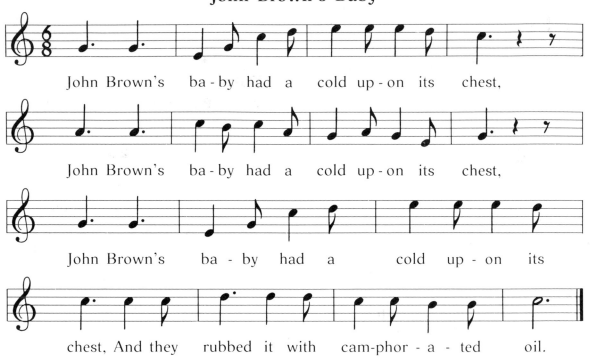

John Brown's ba-by had a cold up-on its chest,

John Brown's ba-by had a cold up-on its chest,

John Brown's ba - by had a cold up - on its

chest, And they rubbed it with cam-phor - a - ted oil.

Do Your Ears Hang Low?

Do your ears hang low? Do they wob-ble to and fro? Can you

tie them in a knot? Can you tie them in a bow? Can you

throw them o-ver your shoul-der Like a con - ti - nen - tal sol-dier? Do your

ears hang low?

The Noble Duke of York

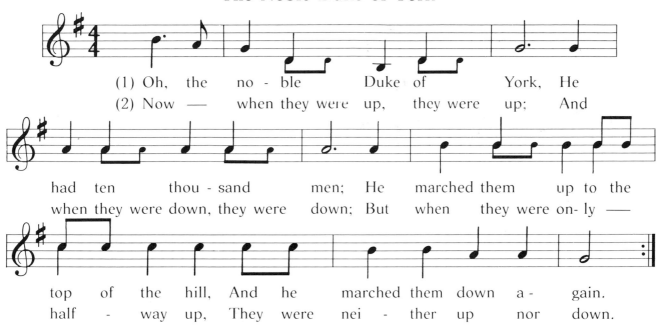

(1) Oh, the no - ble Duke of York, He
(2) Now — when they were up, they were up; And

had ten thou - sand men; He marched them up to the
when they were down, they were down; But when they were on- ly —

top of the hill, And he marched them down a - gain.
half - way up, They were nei - ther up nor down.

The Crocodile

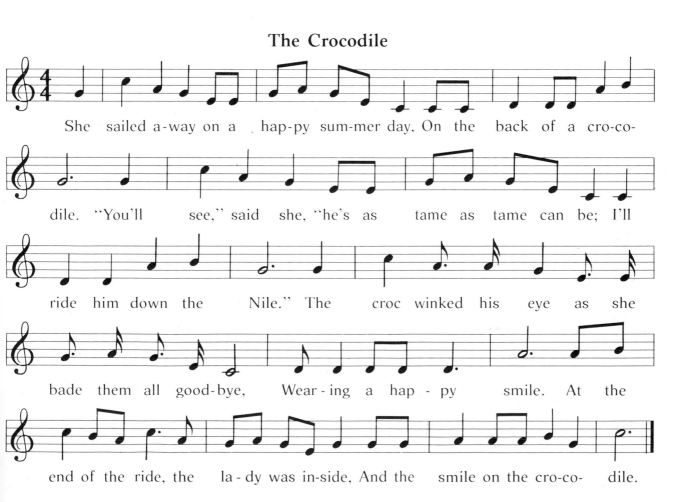

She sailed a-way on a hap-py sum-mer day, On the back of a cro-co-

dile. "You'll see," said she, "he's as tame as tame can be; I'll

ride him down the Nile." The croc winked his eye as she

bade them all good-bye, Wear-ing a hap - py smile. At the

end of the ride, the la - dy was in-side, And the smile on the cro-co- dile.

Wheels on the Bus

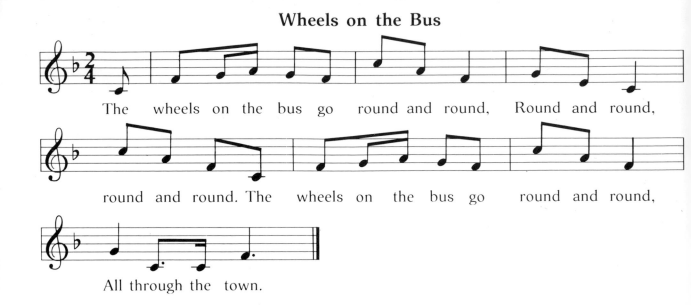

The wheels on the bus go round and round, Round and round,

round and round. The wheels on the bus go round and round,

All through the town.

The driver on the bus says, "Move on back,
Move on back, move on back."
The driver on the bus says, "Move on back,"
All through the town.

The children on the bus say, "Yak yak yak
Yak yak yak, yak yak yak."
The children on the bus say, "Yak yak yak
All through the town.

The mommies on the bus say, "Shh shh shh,
Shh shh shh, shh shh shh."
The mommies on the bus say, "Shh shh shh,"
All through the town.

I'm a Little Teapot

I'm a lit-tle tea-pot, short and stout. Here is my

han-dle, here is my spout. When I start to steam up,

then I shout, Tip me o-ver and pour me out.